GOOD MORNING, MISS GATOR

BY ROBERT KRAUS

Silver Press

Library of Congress Cataloging-in-Publication Data

Kraus, Robert, 1925–
    Good morning, Miss Gator / story and illustrations
by Robert Kraus.
        p.   cm.—(Miss Gator's schoolhouse; bk. 1)
    Summary: Every day Miss Gator goes to the one-
room schoolhouse, where she teaches the young
animals many useful things.
        [1. Schools—Fiction.   2. Alligators—Fiction.
3. Animals—Fiction.]   I. Title.   II. Series: Kraus,
Robert, 1925-   Miss Gator's schoolhouse; bk. 1.
PZ7.K868Gmt   1989
    [E]—dc19   89-6010
                                                        CIP
ISBN 0-671-68605-4 (lib. bdg.)   AC
ISBN 0-671-68609-7 (pbk.)

Produced by Parachute Press, Inc.
Published by Silver Press, a division of
Silver Burdett Press, Inc.
Simon & Schuster, Inc.,
Prentice Hall Bldg., Englewood Cliffs, NJ 07632.
Printed in the United States of America.
10 9 8 7 6 5 4 3 2 1

Chapter 1
ALL ABOUT MISS GATOR

Miss Gator lived alone

in a neat little cabin

in the middle of the

Hokey Smokey Swamp.

She woke up each day
at the crack of dawn
and the crack of her back.

She made herself a good breakfast.

Fresh-squeezed orange juice,

flapjacks and bacon,

six eggs sunny-side up,

grits, toast, and tea.

Start the day with a good breakfast.

That was her motto.

Miss Gator gargled
and gave her teeth
a good brushing.

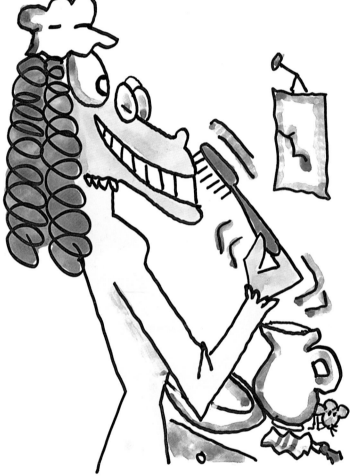

A clean tooth is a happy tooth.
That was another motto.

Then she changed into
her bathing suit
and took a brisk swim.

At 6:35 A.M. she showered

and got dressed.

Now she was ready to face the day.

She hopped into her motorboat.

Zoom!

Off she sped

to the little red schoolhouse

in the swamp.

It was only one room,

but her students got

a heap of learning there.

Miss Gator taught them

the three R's.

Reading, 'riting, and 'rithmetic.

She also taught them all about

sharing, caring, and having fun.

One misty morning, Miss Gator
unlocked the door of the
little red schoolhouse
and went inside.

It was still very early.

So she sat at her hickory desk

and planned the day.

Chapter 2
MISS GATOR'S CLASS

Miss Gator's class began to arrive.

"Good morning, Miss Gator,"

said Ella the Bad Speller.

"Good morning, Ella,"

said Miss Gator.

"Good morning, Miss Gator,"
said Punky Skunky.
"Good morning, Punky,"
said Miss Gator.
Punky was so cute.
She was always dressed in the
latest style.

"Good morning, Miss Gator,"
said Buggy Bear,
scratching his head.
"Good morning, Buggy,"
said Miss Gator.

"Good morning, Miss Gator,"

said Blake the Snake.

"Good morning, Blake,"

said Miss Gator.

It was 8 o'clock.

Time to begin.

But there was still one student

missing.

It was Tardy Toad.

He was always late.

Something would have to be done.

Miss Gator rang the bell.

Clang! Clang! Clang!

Tardy raced through the door.

He tried to slip into his seat

unnoticed.

"You're late again, Tardy,"
said Miss Gator.
"Sorry," said Tardy.
"But I've got a good excuse.
On the way to school,
I was eaten by a lion."

Miss Gator's class roared
with laughter.
"Silence," Miss Gator said.
"Being tardy is bad enough.
But telling fibs is worse!"

Tardy looked down at his feet.

"I was ashamed to say I
overslept," he mumbled.

"Again," hissed Blake the Snake.

"Thank you for telling the truth,
Tardy," said Miss Gator.

"Now let's begin our lessons."

Miss Gator taught the class
how to read.
"Good books make good
friends," she said.

Miss Gator taught the class
how to write.
"If you can't write your name,
you won't know who you are,"
she said.

Then Miss Gator taught the
class arithmetic.

"Learn to add,
or you'll be sad,"
she said.

Then Miss Gator taught Buggy
Bear about cleanliness.

She taught him how to wash
his face.

Miss Gator taught Tardy Toad

how to set his alarm clock

so he would be on time.

The alarm clock went off,

but Tardy slept on.

Miss Gator taught Punky Skunky

how to walk on her toes.

She tried to teach Ella how
to spell.

But Ella was just a bad speller.

And at recess time, Miss Gator
taught Blake the Snake
how to roller skate.

In the afternoon, Miss Gator
served her class juice and cookies.
"Thank you, Miss Gator,"
said the class.
"You're welcome," said Miss Gator.

Chapter 3
GOOD AFTERNOON, MISS GATOR

There was still lots of time

for fun and learning.

Miss Gator taught the class

how to play musical instruments.

Then she taught them
how to draw pictures.
All the students drew
themselves.

At 3 o'clock, Miss Gator
rang the dismissal bell.
"So long," she said.
"So long, Miss Gator,"
said the class.
"We love you."
"I love you, too,"
said Miss Gator.
And she blew them a kiss.

Now all her students were gone.

Miss Gator was all alone.

But not quite.

Tardy Toad was asleep

at his desk.

"Wake up, Tardy, dear,"

said Miss Gator.

"You'll be late getting home."

"Huh? What?" mumbled Tardy.

Then he woke up

and dashed out the door.

Miss Gator sat at her desk
in the empty schoolhouse.
She was tired, but happy.
She loved to teach.
But now it was time to go home.

Miss Gator got into her
motorboat and sped
across the swamp.
Tomorrow was another day.